Adapted by Catherine Hapka

Based on the character "Air Bud" created by Kevin DiCicco

Based on characters created by Paul Tamasy & Aaron Mendelsohn

Spooky Buddies is based on the screenplay written by Robert Vince and Anna McRoberts

DISNEY PRESS

New York

Printed in the United States of America
First Edition
1 3 5 7 9 10 8 6 4 2
J689-1817-1-11166
ISBN 978-1-4231-3771-9
For more Disney Press fun, visit www.disneybooks.com

Chapter One

Fernfield, USA
Halloween night, 1937

It was a dark and stormy night. Lightning sparked across the sky. An owl named Hoot flew toward a large Victorian manor on the outskirts of town.

Hoot glided through a window of the manor's tallest turret. Inside stood a man in dark robes. He held a staff with a large black jewel at the top.

"Tonight is the night," the man said as Hoot landed on a perch beside him. "All Hallows' Eve, and the moon is full. I'll show those fools how powerful Warwick the Warlock really is!"

"Master, you are the evilest," Hoot said in approval.

Five beagle puppies sat at Warwick's feet. One of the puppies, Pip, stepped forward.

"Excuse me, Mr. Hoot, sir," Pip said politely. "When do we get to meet the Howlloween Hound?"

"I think Master is almost ready," Hoot replied.

Warwick touched a candlestick, and a secret panel in the wall slid open.

Behind it were shelves of potions and a large leather-bound book.

Meanwhile, several cars arrived outside. Sheriff Jim jumped out of one, along with his loyal bloodhound, Deputy Tracker. More townspeople got out of the other cars.

One was a seven-year-old boy named Joseph. His father was with him. "Pip!" Joseph called through the tall iron gates. "We have to find him, Dad! He's my best friend!" Five puppies had gone missing, and Joseph's puppy, Pip, was one of them. The sheriff and Deputy Tracker's detective work had led them to the manor.

Deputy Tracker was sniffing around. He picked up a scent almost immediately and let out a howl.

Sheriff Jim looked up. A light was burning in the mansion's highest turret.

"That no-good Warwick must have the puppies!" the sheriff said. He pulled at the chain on the gate. "Give me a hand with this."

As the sheriff tried to break open the chain, Warwick heard the commotion and looked out the window. "Drat," he muttered when he saw the intruders cutting the chain. "We'd better hurry," he said to Hoot.

A tall mirror stood nearby. Warwick stepped in front of it. It was time to recite one of the spells from his leather-bound book. The gem on his staff began to glow as he spoke:

"On All Hallows' Eve,
When the moon is full and bright,
Open a portal to beyond the light.
Call three times to summon
A hound with great might.
The souls of five puppies
Will be yours this night."

"Master," Hoot said, "what do you mean about 'souls being his'?" That didn't sound right to Hoot.

"Silence, you birdbrain!" Warwick ordered.

The gem on his staff burned with an otherworldly light. He pointed it toward the mirror.

"Howlloween Hound, Howlloween Hound, Howlloween Hound!" he cried.

A beam of moonlight hit the gem, then the mirror. The mirror glowed, causing a mysterious light to swirl around the room.

In the glass, a new reflection was forming. Large. Dark. Scary. Canine.

Warwick smiled. "Come to our side, Howlloween Hound!"

The shape solidified. "Who summons me?" a deep voice howled from within the mirror.

Warwick took a step back. He couldn't help feeling a little nervous.

"I have, Hound," he answered. "Warwick the Great! I have five puppy souls of the same blood who are *dying* to meet you. I believe that is what you need to open the portal."

"Why should I open the portal for you?" the Hound growled.

"With your help, we will unleash all creatures of the underworld into Fernfield!" Warwick declared. "You and I can rule the land, Hound!"

"I like the sound of that," the Hound said.

"We must hurry," Warwick warned. "We only have this night, Halloween, while the moon is full." He glanced at the puppies. "You can meet the Howlloween Hound now," he told them with a sinister smile.

Suddenly, the Hound let out a loud howl. Magical energy poured out of his mouth. It swirled around one of the puppies. . . .

Outside, Sheriff Jim had broken through the gate. Now he tried the front door. It was locked.

"Grab that tree trunk," he told the others. "We'll have to knock down the door."

"Pip, where are you?" Joseph cried.

High above in the turret, Pip was now the only puppy left. The others had been turned to stone by the Howlloween Hound. He had taken their souls!

"Mr. Hoot, I changed my mind," Pip said. "I don't want to go with the Howlloween Hound. I just want to be with my boy!"

"Master," the owl said, "the puppy doesn't want to go now."

Warwick ignored the owl. He reached for Pip.

But Pip didn't trust him. He bit Warwick's finger, then took off.

"Ow!" Warwick yelped. "Why you little—"

He chased the puppy down the manor's grand staircase.

Just then, the door burst open. Townspeople poured in, including Joseph.

"Pip!" the little boy cried.

He reached for his puppy. But Warwick swooped in and grabbed Pip first.

"Stay back!" the warlock warned, pulling out a potion bottle. "Or I'll turn you all into toads!"

Two men ignored him and stepped forward. Warwick splashed the potion on them.

POOF!

The men vanished. Their clothes fell to the floor. A second later, two toads hopped out! Everyone gasped as Warwick flew up the stairs with Pip.

Joseph pulled away from his father and ran after the warlock. He had to save his puppy!

Warwick raced upstairs. "Quickly, Hound, take that last puppy!" he urged when he reached the turret. "Complete the spell—now!"

The Hound howled. Pip couldn't get away this time. He slowly turned to stone as his spirit floated up out of his body toward the mirror.

"Pip!" Joseph cried, bursting through the door.

The sheriff's dog, Deputy Tracker, raced in. Leaping at Warwick, he grabbed the magic staff in his teeth.

"Hey!" Warwick yelled. "Let go!"

At that moment, the first rays of sunlight poured in through the window. A beam hit the jewel on Warwick's staff. The jewel's glow faded away.

Warwick gasped. No! His spell had to be completed by dawn, or the Hound would remain in the mirror and Warwick wouldn't be able to take over the town.

"Hound! Wait!" he cried. "Open the portal!"

But the Hound's image was fading. Even though he'd already turned Pip to stone, he hadn't had time to finish taking the puppy's soul before dawn broke. It was too late.

"I need all five puppy souls. . . ." The Hound's growl trailed off. A moment later, his image faded away.

By then, Sheriff Jim and Joseph's dad had arrived. "It's over, Warwick!" Sheriff Jim said. "Enough of your black magic—this town will not stand for it!"

Warwick backed away. "I'll take over this town one day!" he declared. "Mark my words, I will return!"

Then he dove into the mirror, disappearing as the glow faded completely.

Joseph ran to the stone statue of Pip. "Dad," he cried, "look what they did to Pip! We need to turn Pip back!"

"He's gone, Joseph," his father said

sadly. "Pip's gone. Let's go home, son."

Joseph couldn't believe he had lost his puppy. He walked sadly out of the room.

But Pip wasn't gone. Not entirely. His spirit was still hovering overhead, watching everything.

"Joseph?" Pip said. "Wait! I'm right here!"

But the humans and Deputy Tracker were already leaving. They hurried downstairs and out the front door. When Pip tried to follow them outside, he found himself blocked by some invisible force.

"No!" the puppy cried.

Outside, Joseph hugged the stone puppy his dad had given him. "Poor Pip," Joseph said.

"What happened, Sheriff?" one of the townspeople asked.

Sheriff Jim was still holding Warwick's staff. Joseph's dad had the spell book.

"I don't know," the sheriff said. "But this home is officially condemned. Let's board it up—I don't want anyone going in."

As they got back into their cars, nobody noticed the owl flying out the turret window.

"I will wait for you to return, Master," Hoot promised.

Chapter Two

Fernfield, USA
October 31, present day

"No one is exactly sure what happened that night—or if the legend is even true," Mrs. Carroll said. "But it's an interesting part of Fernfield folklore."

Her class stared at the boarded-up old manor on the outskirts of town. Five of the kids in the class—Billy, Pete, Bartleby, Sam, and Alice—were there.

They had brought their golden retriever puppies with them—B-Dawg, Mudbud, Budderball, Buddha, and Rosebud. Together, the five pups were known as the Buddies. They were tagging along on the class's Spooky Fernfield field trip.

One of the bigger kids in the class, Rodney, looked around with a smirk. "Tell that to the kids who got eaten by the Howlloween Hound last year," he said. "Kids go in every Halloween and say the Hound's name in the mirror three times, and they're never seen again!"

Suddenly, there was a loud howl from the bushes. Everyone gasped.

A boy named Skip stepped out. He

was the one who had howled. He laughed and traded high fives with Rodney.

"Okay, Rodney and Skip," Mrs. Carroll scolded. "There will be no more tricks. Come along children, we have two more stops on our Spooky Fernfield tour."

As the kids climbed on the bus, the Buddies started to follow. Then the puppies noticed that one of their group was missing.

"Where's B-Dawg hiding?" Buddha wondered.

B-Dawg stepped out from behind some bushes. "I wasn't hiding, yo," he said. "I was just getting ready to pounce on that Hound."

"Sure, dude," Mudbud said. "You

were hiding like a scaredy cat, 'cause you thought there was a ghost."

"B-Dawg is afraid of nothing!" B-Dawg bragged. He liked to think he was the toughest of the Buddies. "I'll prove it— I'll go in there right now, call out that Howlloween Hound, and kick his tail."

He raced off toward the house. The other puppies chased after him.

B-Dawg slipped inside the house past an opening in the wood, and the rest of the Buddies followed.

"See? It's . . . it's not too scary," B-Dawg said, trying to sound brave. But the place was definitely spooky. Everything was covered in dust and cobwebs. Only a little light seeped in through the boards on the windows. "I'm going to prove once and for all that I ain't no scaredy cat."

B-Dawg headed toward the stairs.

"Uh, okay," Rosebud said. "You're not a scaredy cat. We take it back."

But B-Dawg kept going. Reluctantly, the other Buddies followed him up the stairs. None of them noticed the ghost puppy floating along above them. . . .

Mrs. Carroll's class got off the bus at the Fernfield cemetery. "Many people and their pets from Fernfield history have their final resting place here," the teacher said.

The kids looked around nervously.

"I could do without the cemetery on Halloween," Billy said. He was not feeling very good about this.

The others nodded in agreement. But Mrs. Carroll led them farther in.

"Here's the great Deputy Tracker's grave," she pointed out. "One of the best canine officers our town ever saw."

Billy looked at the grave site. Beside it was a statue of a cute little beagle puppy. What was that doing there?

Then he heard the sound of a shovel hitting dirt. Looking around, he saw a tall, gloomy old man digging a grave.

"Good afternoon, Mr. Johnson," Mrs. Carroll said to the old man. She turned to her students. "That's the caretaker," she told them. "He's been running this place as long as I can remember."

"That dude is spook central!" Pete

whispered to his friends as the class continued on its way.

Back at the manor, B-Dawg had reached the turret room. He looked around and spotted four stone puppy statues. He shivered slightly. Then he stared into the dark mirror.

"Just say it three times, and it will all be over," he whispered to himself. He knew this was the only way to prove he wasn't scared.

The other Buddies entered the room. And so did the ghost puppy! It was Pip, who had been trapped in the manor all those years by himself. He couldn't believe that other puppies were actually there. But the only one of the Buddies who caught a glimpse of the ghostly beagle pup was Budderball.

"Did you guys just see that?" he asked nervously.

"See what?" Mudbud asked.

Budderball was still looking up, but Pip had disappeared. "A strange glow," he said. "Like a ghost. Maybe we ought to just leave."

"Look who's a scaredy cat, now," B-Dawg teased. He took a deep breath. "Howlloween Hound . . ."

"Okay, nothing happened," Budderball interrupted. "Let's go!"

"Howlloween Hound," B-Dawg said again.

Pip flew in front of B-Dawg. "Don't say it, please!" he cried.

This time all the Buddies saw the ghost. They froze in terror.

"Stop!" Pip urged. "Don't say it again! You'll release them!"

B-Dawg couldn't believe his eyes. "You're . . . you're the H-H-Howlloween Hound!" he cried.

"Oh, no!" Pip exclaimed as the mirror started to glow. "You said it three times!"

The Buddies were already racing out of the room. Pip flew after them.

"Wait!" he cried. "I'm not the Howlloween Hound!"

But the Buddies didn't hear him. They ran out of the house without looking back.

Chapter Three

Hoot the owl had been waiting for his master all these years, just as he'd promised. Now he watched as five puppies burst out of the old manor and raced for the gate.

Excited, he flew after them, landing silently on the gate so he could hear what they said.

"That was a ghost, dawgs!" B-Dawg exclaimed. "A real off-the-chain ghoul!"

"Maybe we imagined it," Rosebud said uncertainly. "It was pretty spooky in there."

"It looked totally real to me, dudette," Mudbud said. "Was it the Howlloween Hound?"

"I said Howlloween Hound three times into the mirror, dawgs," B-Dawg reminded the group. "I released the Howlloween Hound! You guys all saw him, too!"

"Whatever it was," Budderball said with a nervous glance at the house, "we are outta there."

"Come on, let's catch up to our kids," Buddha said.

With that, the puppies ran off.

* * *

25

The kids' class trip ended at Fernfield Town Hall. The place was decorated for Halloween with spooky cobwebs, carved pumpkins, fake tombstones, flapping rubber bats, and more.

"All right, kids," Mrs. Carroll said. "That concludes the field trip. Now, I know you're all excited about trick-or-treating tonight, but let's not forget that your Fernfield history projects are due Monday."

Most of the students nodded. But Billy's eyes went wide. He'd forgotten all about that project!

"Monday?" he asked.

Rodney and Skip laughed.

"What a bonehead!" Rodney jeered.

Mrs. Carroll gave the pair a stern

look. "Yes, Billy," she replied. "It's been assigned for two weeks. You'll have all weekend for the finishing touches. What subject did you choose?"

"Uh . . ." Billy began. Then he said the first thing that came into his head: "The curse of the Howlloween Hound."

"Certainly a good topic for this time of year," Mrs. Carroll said. "Class dismissed! I hope to see you all at my house tonight for treats. Happy Halloween!"

As most of the students scurried off, Alice, Bartleby, Pete, and Sam gathered around Billy. He looked anxious.

"Come on," Alice said, trying to cheer him up. Researching the mystery of the Howlloween Hound would be fun! "If the police were involved, I bet

Sheriff Dan knows a thing or two."

Alice's friends knew she was probably right, so they went to the town hall and found Sheriff Dan. When they explained that they wanted to know about the Howlloween Hound, the sheriff led them down into the basement.

The basement was dim and dusty. Every inch of it was crammed with old boxes and stacks of files. Billy looked around and spotted a box with a label that read: HALLOWEEN, 1937.

"Good detective work, Billy," Sheriff Dan said as he pulled out a thick file and handed it to the boy.

"Thanks, Sheriff," Billy said. Then he noticed something interesting stuck behind the box. It was a long staff with a jewel on the top. "Whoa . . . that would be awesome for my presentation. Can I borrow it?"

"I suppose it couldn't hurt. But remember, it's still police evidence, so I'll need it back." Sheriff Dan chuckled. "And don't go casting any spells. I wouldn't want to end up a toad!"

Chapter Four

Billy rushed into his house with B-Dawg at his heels. The Buddies had caught up to the kids at the town hall. Then all of them had headed home to get ready for trick-or-treating.

"Hey, Mom," Billy said as he burst into the kitchen.

Billy's mom looked up from frosting cookies. "Hello, dear. I'm just finishing up my famous jack-o'-lantern cookies for tonight's Spooky Brew-Ha-Ha."

The Spooky Brew-Ha-Ha was the town's annual Halloween party. Most of the adults in Fernfield were planning to go while the kids went trick-or-treating.

"Did you pick up my costume?" Billy asked.

"Sure did. It's on the table. And I got a matching one for B-Dawg!"

Billy walked over to check out his costume. He gasped in horror. It was a powder blue bunny suit, and there was one for B-Dawg, too!

He couldn't trick-or-treat as a silly bunny! What was he going to do?

He glanced at the staff he was holding. Hmm . . .

Rushing upstairs, Billy dug into his closet. Finally, he found a dark blue robe in the back.

He pulled on the robe and held up the staff. "What do you think, B-Dawg? Warwick the Warlock at your service!"

While Billy was busy, B-Dawg had pulled on the bunny costume. He whined with dismay when he looked at himself.

"Sorry, B-Dawg," Billy said. Then he pulled out the case file the sheriff had given him. He flipped through the papers until he found a couple of pictures. One was a police sketch of Warwick. The other was a very old photo of a boy and a beagle puppy.

"Look, B-Dawg," Billy said. "This must

be what the warlock looked like. And the photo must be the boy from the story—and his pup, Pip." He noticed a number on the house in the second picture. "'1114 Pine Lane,'" he read. "I wonder if he still lives there?"

B-Dawg barked.

"Yeah, it was over seventy years ago," Billy said. "He'd be older than grandma by now! But if I could talk to him, this would be the easiest project ever!"

There was no time to think about that just then. Billy stuck the photo in his pocket and put the rest of the stuff into his backpack.

"Trick-or-treating time," he told B-Dawg. "We'd better fly!"

* * *

Meanwhile, two of Billy's classmates were thinking more about *tricks* than *treats*. Rodney and Skip stood at the door of the old manor. Rodney tried to pry at the boards on the door with a crowbar.

"Hurry!" Skip whispered.

"There!" Rodney said as one of the boards finally broke.

A loud wail sounded behind them. Skip spun around, his heart pounding. A black cat glared at him.

"Chill, it's just a dumb cat," Rodney said. "Come on, I bet there's tons of weird stuff in here we can use to scare those dweebs from class."

He squeezed in past the broken board. Skip followed.

Inside, Pip saw the two boys enter. Floating, he hid behind a chandelier as Skip shone a flashlight around.

"This way," Rodney said as he started up the staircase.

The sun was setting as the two boys reached the turret room. Rodney wandered around, checking it out. He picked up a dusty old candlestick . . . and part of the wall slid aside. It was a secret hiding place! "Awesome!" Rodney exclaimed.

Skip stared at the mirror. Was it his imagination, or was it . . . glowing?

"Rodney," he said.

Rodney barely heard him. He was looking at the potion bottles in the secret compartment. The labels were hard to read.

" 'Rodent-trans'…something," Rodney muttered.

Pip was watching from overhead. He noticed the full moon rising outside. Then, a moonbeam drifted into the room and hit the mirror.

"Oh, no . . ." Pip whispered.

"Rodney!" Skip cried.

Rodney finally turned around—just in time to see Warwick stumble out of the mirror!

"We're free!" Warwick cried. "It was horrendous in there." Suddenly he noticed the two boys gaping at him. "You there! Are you the ones who released us? Where's my staff? And my book? You've stolen them, haven't you?"

Rodney and Skip were too scared

to answer. Behind Warwick, the Hound appeared in the mirror. He stepped out into the room, too.

"Come on, Hound. We must find my things. We have to complete the spell tonight." He saw the potion bottle in Rodney's hands and grabbed it from him. *"Rodentus transformus!"* he chanted.

Then, without warning, he splashed the potion onto Rodney and Skip. The two boys disappeared—and a moment later, a pair of rats popped out of their clothes!

Warwick smiled. "Now they won't be able to warn the town."

Just then, Hoot flew in. "Master, it's true!" the owl cried. "You've been called forth!"

"Yes, Hoot," Warwick said with an evil grin. "I've finally been freed from the mirror. We must complete the spell!"

"Five puppies of the same blood," the Hound growled, reminding the Warlock what they needed.

"Five puppies from the same blood just released you," Hoot told his master.

"Where are they now?" Warwick demanded.

"I'm not exactly sure," Hoot replied, looking around.

Warwick rolled his eyes. "Of course you're not. Still as much of a birdbrain as ever!"

None of them saw Pip, who was still

hiding and watching. He realized that Hoot was talking about the Buddies!

Warwick and the Hound hurried outside. Hoot flew down to join them.

"First we must find my staff," Warwick said. "Nothing can happen without it. Hoot, fly ahead and look. It will be illuminated by the full moon."

"Yes, Master!" Hoot flew off.

Then Warwick ordered the Hound to go look for the puppies.

Pip watched from the window. He wasn't sure what to do. Then he thought of something. "If they can leave, maybe I can, too!" he whispered.

He floated one ghostly paw toward the door, waiting for that invisible shield to stop him as it had before. But nothing happened! "I'm not trapped anymore!" he cried as he flew outside. "Woo-hoo!" he said excitedly. Then he got down to business. "Okay, I'd better find those puppies. . . ."

Chapter Five

The Buddies and their kids met outside Billy's house. All of them were in costume. Alice was dressed as a witch, and her puppy, Rosebud, as a princess. Sam was an alien, and his puppy, Buddha, was a genie. Pete was a mummy, and his puppy, Mudbud, was a pirate. Bartleby was a cowboy, and his puppy, Budderball, was a superhero.

Then, there were Billy and B-Dawg.

"Nice costume, matey." Mudbud giggled. "Does the *B* stand for bunny?"

B-Dawg tried to play it cool. "This ain't no ordinary rabbit costume, dawgs," he said. "It's a *killer* rabbit. Those things are da' bomb!"

Billy held up his staff, pretending to be Warwick. "With the Howlloween Hound, I'll control the world! Ha-ha-ha!" he cried, doing his best evil laugh.

"Hey, that was really good," Bartleby said. "Now let's go score some sugar!"

The friends and their pups set out into the streets of Fernfield. Lots of other kids were trick-or-treating, too. Most of the houses were draped with spooky decorations. The full moon shone brightly in the dark night sky.

Alice glanced at Billy's staff. "Is that thing glowing?" she asked.

Billy looked at it curiously. Strangely enough, it *was* glowing. Weird.

"Uh, maybe it has batteries or something?" Billy said. He shrugged, and he and his friends continued on.

With the Buddies in tow, they walked toward their teacher's house. It had more decorations than any other house in town. There were tombstones on the lawn and cobwebs in the trees. A mechanical ghost flew in circles above them.

The kids knocked on the door. Mrs. Carroll's husband answered. He was dressed as a surfer version of Frankenstein's monster.

"Trick-or-treat!" the kids sang out.

"Dude, sweet costume!" Pete added.

"That's *Frankendude* to you!" Mr. Carroll replied.

Mrs. Carroll rushed up behind her husband. She was dressed as the Bride of Frankendude.

"Hello, children! Welcome to our spoooooooky house!" she said. Then she and her husband handed out candy to the kids and dog biscuits to the Buddies.

"Oh, sweet mama!" Budderball exclaimed. "Why can't it be Halloween every night?"

In another part of town, Pip was searching for the Buddies. He had to warn them about Warwick!

As he floated along, he was amazed

by what he saw. "I'm not alone!" he exclaimed. "There are ghosts and goblins everywhere!"

But then he took a closer look and noticed some of the ghosts and goblins adjusting their masks and costumes. "They're not real," he realized.

He didn't want to scare anyone. He found a sheet someone had dropped from their ghost costume, and draped it over himself as a disguise. Then he floated down the street.

Soon he spotted five familiar forms—the Buddies! He sped toward them, still covered by the sheet.

"Thank goodness I found you!" he cried. "I'm here to warn you about the Howlloween Hound."

"How did you know about that?" Rosebud asked.

Pip pulled off the sheet, revealing his true form. B-Dawg screamed.

"*Aaaah!* It's the Howlloween Hound! He's following us!" he yelled.

"*Aaaah!*" the other Buddies screamed. And they all raced away.

"Not again!" Pip exclaimed. "Please, wait! I'm just trying to warn you!"

He flew after them.

"This ghost dawg just doesn't give up!" B-Dawg cried. "What do we do?"

"I know a place," Buddha suggested. "If there's anyone who can help us with a paranormal problem, it's Zelda."

The Buddies were all so distracted they didn't notice that they'd rushed right past the real Howlloween Hound. But the Howlloween Hound noticed the Buddies. He'd been sniffing all around town for those five puppies.

His spooky eyes narrowed as he watched the Buddies hurry off. "That must be them," he growled.

Chapter Six

A few blocks away, Warwick walked down a different street. A group of trick-or-treaters came toward him. Most of the kids were dressed as goblins, skeletons, or other scary creatures. One girl was dressed as a fairy princess.

"Hurry up!" the fairy princess called to her dad, who was walking behind the group of kids she was with. "The best candy is on the next street!"

The kids hurried forward, with the girl's dad rushing to keep up.

Warwick shuddered. "That pink goblin was hideous!" he said. "This is dreadful. Evil creatures are roaming the streets and controlling the townsfolk. Someone has beaten us to it—this town has already been taken over!"

Warwick couldn't believe it. He'd spent more than seventy years looking forward to taking over Fernfield himself.

But maybe he still could. He knew he would first have to find Hoot and the Hound—and then act fast.

Hoot was soaring above the town, watching for the glow of his master's staff. Finally he spotted it. Yes! The

Warlock would be pleased with him.

Billy and his friends didn't notice the owl landing in a tree nearby. They'd just stopped in front of a darkened house. It was the only one on the block without any decorations.

"Remind me never to come trick-or-treating here," Bartleby said. He peered at the address on the house. "At . . . 1114 Pine Lane. Talk about no Halloween spirit!"

"1114 Pine Lane?" Billy repeated. He pulled out the photograph he had stuck in his pocket. "Hey! The boy from the story lived here. This was Joseph's house!"

"Go knock on the door, Billy," Alice urged. "Maybe he still lives here."

"He'd be, like, a thousand years old," Billy replied. But he walked up to the house and rang the doorbell anyway.

Nobody answered. Billy turned back toward the others, who were waiting on the sidewalk.

"I guess nobody's home," Billy told them.

But just then, the door opened behind him. The other kids gasped as someone stepped out. It was Mr. Johnson, the spooky old man from the cemetery!

"Look behind you!" Sam whispered loudly, pointing.

"Ha-ha, good one," Billy said. "I'm not falling for . . ."

He trailed off when he noticed his friends' faces. They all looked pretty scared. What if they weren't joking?

Slowly, he turned around. Mr. Johnson glared down at him.

Billy gulped. "Um . . . hello . . . sir," he stammered. "I was wondering if this boy still lives here."

His hand shook as he held up the photo of Joseph. Mr. Johnson looked at it.

"No," Mr. Johnson said sharply. "This boy hasn't lived here in quite some time. Every year a kid like you comes asking about that story. Why can't you leave it alone? Now go away!"

"Okay," Billy said immediately. "Sorry, sir."

As he backed away, Mr. Johnson noticed the staff Billy was holding. It glowed softly in the moonlight.

"Where did you get that, boy?" Mr. Johnson snapped. "Hand it over! It's very dangerous!"

He grabbed for the staff, but Billy pulled away just in time.

"*Aaaaah!*" Billy yelled. "Run!"

He and his friends raced away as fast as they could.

Hoot observed the scene for a moment more. Then he flapped his wings and took off, the full moon lighting his way.

Warwick was still wandering around town. "Where is that useless owl?" he muttered.

He watched as a group of kids went to the door of Mrs. Carroll's house.

Mr. Carroll, dressed as Frankendude, answered and passed out candy.

"All the goblins and ghouls are flocking to his door," Warwick noted. That must mean there was some evil going on at the house. Warwick needed to find out. He waited until the kids left, then knocked on the door himself.

Mr. Carroll looked surprised when he answered. "Aren't you a little old to be trick-or-treating?"

"No," Warwick said. "Now give me what rightfully belongs to me!"

Just then Hoot arrived. He flew down and landed on Warwick's arm.

"Master," the owl said, "I have good news."

Frankendude stared at the talking

owl. "Oh, I get it!" he said. "You're a ventriloquist. Very impressive."

He gave Warwick a candy bar, then shut the door. Warwick stared at the candy. The sorcerer had said it was a treat, so he decided to take a bite. He didn't realize it was still in the wrapper.

Yuck! He spit it out.

"This is what they call food these days?" Warwick complained. "Now what's this good news, Hoot? Have you found my staff?"

"Yes. A young warlock has it," Hoot replied.

Warwick frowned. "I leave for seventy-five measly years and someone tries to replace me! Where's the respect?" With a grunt, he followed Hoot.

Chapter Seven

"This way, Master," Hoot said, leading the way.

The owl flapped along the street. Warwick looked ahead and spotted Billy holding *his* staff. And Billy wasn't alone.

"He's got all sorts of terrifying creatures following him," Warwick commented with disgust. "How will we get to him?"

The warlock couldn't waste any more time. He needed to get his staff back and then move on with his plan. He walked up to Billy.

"Young warlock," he addressed the boy, "do you know who I am?"

Billy and his friends looked confused. "Uh, I'm not sure," Billy said.

"I am Warwick the Warlock!" Warwick declared. "The most evil warlock known to man! All you ghouls will be my slaves! Now give me my staff."

Billy's eyes widened. Now he knew why this guy looked familiar. He'd seen his picture in that police file!

Warwick lunged for the staff. Billy did the only thing he could think of—he pointed the staff at Warwick.

"Protect us!" he commanded in his best wizard voice.

The staff lit up. Warwick gasped. "Oh, no!" he cried.

A second later a bolt of magical energy shot out of the staff. It hit Warwick, sending him flying back. He landed in a fake coffin on someone's lawn, and the coffin's lid slammed shut.

"Whoa," Billy said, completely shocked.

"How did you *do* that?" Sam asked, equally shocked.

Billy shook his head. "I have no idea. But look at this!" He pulled the police sketch out of his backpack and showed it to the others.

"Dudes!" Pete exclaimed, "he really is the warlock!"

"Let's go find Sheriff Dan," Alice added. *"Now!"*

They all took off. A moment later, the coffin's lid flipped open. Hoot landed on a nearby fake tombstone and peered down into the coffin.

"Are you okay, Master?" he asked.

Warwick sat up. He didn't look okay. The magical bolt had frizzed his hair. His robe was smoldering.

"I clearly underestimated that warlock," he muttered, glaring down the street after the kids.

Warwick picked himself up. He smoothed down his hair and shook the ashes from his robe. Determined to make things right, he returned to Mrs. Carroll's door with Hoot perched on his arm. Once again, Mr. Carroll answered.

"Oh, hey," Mr. Carroll said. "Loved

your bit. But everyone only gets one piece of candy per trick."

"I need your help, monster," Warwick said with narrowed eyes. "You're big and scary and the perfect henchman for the job." Then, without warning, Warlock pulled out a potion and splashed it on Mr. Carroll.

"Servis mentus!" Warwick chanted.

Mr. Carroll's eyes suddenly turned green.

"You will now do exactly as I say," Warwick commanded.

"Yes, Master," Mr. Carroll responded. He was hypnotized.

Warwick smiled. Finally, something was going right. "I want you to find a young warlock carrying a staff with a

Inside an old manor, Warwick the Warlock and
the Howlloween Hound are plotting to
turn Fernfield evil.

The Howlloween Hound needs Pip's soul
before he can escape from the magical mirror.

"Look what they did to Pip!" Joseph cries.
The Hound turned his puppy to stone!
Only Pip's ghost is left behind.

Mrs. Carroll tells her class the story of Joseph
and Pip. "No one is exactly sure what
happened that night."

B-Dawg is not happy about his Halloween costume—but he's ready for some trick-or-treating.

More than seventy years later, Warwick and the Howlloween Hound have returned to take over Fernfield!

After the Buddies explore Warwick's old manor, they realize that Pip's ghost is following them!

"This is Halloween, the only night spirits are free to roam," Zelda tells the Buddies.

Warwick knows Billy has his magic staff,
so he chases after the kids.

The Fernfield cemetery's caretaker, Mr. Johnson,
saves the kids just in time. But they must
stop Warwick.

At the cemetery, the Buddies find Pip's grave, and Zelda returns his spirit to his body.

Warwick and the Hound have trapped the Buddies in the old manor!

In the nick of time, B-Dawg comes up with
a plan and saves all the puppies.

Billy recites a spell from Warwick's spell book
and sends the evil warlock back into the
magical mirror!

The kids are so excited to be reunited
with their puppies!

Mr. Johnson reveals that he is Pip's friend Joseph.
He is happy to have his puppy back after
all these years.

glowing black jewel," he said. "Seize it—
and eliminate him."

"Yes, Master," Mr. Carroll replied.

He stepped off the porch. His foot
landed right in a jack-o'-lantern, but he
kept walking with the pumpkin stuck on
his foot.

Then Warwick and Hoot followed
Frankendude out of the yard.

Chapter Eight

Meanwhile, the Buddies wandered down Main Street. "I think we lost him," Rosebud said, looking behind her.

"Why is that ghost dude after us?" Mudbud wondered.

B-Dawg shrugged. "Maybe he wants to drink our blood."

"That's vampires," Rosebud told him.

"Maybe he wants to eat our brains," B-Dawg suggested.

Rosebud sighed. "That's zombies."

"Maybe he wants to devour everything he sees," B-Dawg said.

"That's Budderball," Rosebud replied.

Mudbud was still thinking about his question. "It's probably because B-Dawg released it from the mirror," he said.

"Oh, sure, dawg, blame me!" B-Dawg exclaimed.

The puppies continued down the street thinking they had gotten rid of Pip. But little did they know that they hadn't lost the ghost at all! He was still floating behind them, dressed in his sheet costume.

Finally the Buddies arrived at a darkened store. The sign over the door identified it as the Fernfield Shop of Curiosities.

The puppies looked up nervously, and Buddha led the way inside through a doggy door. The place was filled with all sorts of mystical stuff—beads, incense, tarot cards, and other oddities.

"Hello?" Buddha called out. "Is anyone home?"

"Check out this crystal ball," Budderball said, spotting a large glass orb on a table.

Buddha was still looking for his friend. "Zelda?" he called out.

Suddenly the image of a dog appeared in the crystal ball. "Who wants to know?" a voice asked.

"*Aaaah!*" B-Dawg cried. "The gumball is talking to us!"

"It's me, Buddha," Buddha said to the dog in the crystal ball, "and my brothers and sister. The Buddies."

Suddenly, a head popped out from behind the crystal ball. It was Buddha's friend Zelda, a Chinese crested dog dressed as a gypsy. She hadn't been *inside* the crystal, merely *behind* it!

"Welcome," she said to the puppies. "I am Zelda. I am all-knowing and all-seeing. I specialize in the mystic and otherworldly."

"We need your help," Buddha told her urgently. "This ghost has been chasing us."

Zelda nodded. "This is Halloween, the only night spirits are free to roam," she replied. "We must make contact with this ghost of yours."

Just then, Pip floated in through the wall. Budderball's eyes widened. "There's the ghost!" he said, pointing at Pip.

Zelda looked at Pip. *"Ghost?!"* she cried. Then she fainted.

The Buddies all froze in terror as Pip floated toward them.

"Please," Pip begged them. "I'm not going to hurt you."

"That's what ghosts always say before they eat you," B-Dawg said.

"Ghosts don't eat," Pip told him.

Budderball's eyes went wide. "That's the saddest thing I've ever heard!"

Suddenly, Zelda stirred. Then she woke up. When she saw Pip, she shrieked again. But this time she didn't pass out.

"I know I look strange," Pip told everyone. "But I was once a pup just like you all. My name is Pip."

Buddha gasped. He remembered the kids' class trip. "You're the pup from the story?" he asked in disbelief.

"Yes. I've been like this ever since that night. The Hound did this to me."

"The spell must have been interrupted," Zelda said in amazement. "You were left in limbo."

"I'm sorry I scared you guys at the manor," Pip told the Buddies. "I was trying to stop you from releasing the Hound."

"We're sorry, too, Pip," Rosebud said.

"The Hound and Warwick are free," Pip told everyone. "They're still trying to finish their spell, and they need five puppies of the same blood to do it. They have their sights set on you five."

"We must stop them!" Zelda declared. "And Pip, now that you have left the manor, if you do not return to your body before sunrise, you will be lost forever. We must find your corporeal self."

"My *what*?" Pip asked.

"The body you once inhabited. We shall ask my crystal ball." Zelda turned to the crystal ball. "Please show us this young pup's body. Does it still exist on the earthly plane?"

The crystal ball started to glow. Then an image formed within it. It was the stone statue of Pip.

"That's me!" Pip cried. "I turned to

stone the night it all happened."

"And where does this body now reside?" Zelda asked the crystal ball.

It formed another image. "Oh, snap! The cemetery!" B-Dawg exclaimed. Then he let out a small whimper. "Do we really have to go back there, dawgs?"

Suddenly, the doggy door to the shop flapped open, and the Howlloween Hound stuck his huge head in!

"Come out, puppies!" He growled. "I'll have all your souls for dinner!"

"*Aaah!* It's the real Howlloween Hound!" B-Dawg cried.

The Hound growled evilly and tried to push himself through the doggy door.

"The back door!" Zelda cried. "Quickly!"

Pip flew through the wall, while the Buddies and Zelda ducked through another doggy door. The Buddies didn't dare look behind them as they ran away. Phew! They'd escaped from the Hound. For now. . . .

Chapter Nine

The Halloween Brew-Ha-Ha party was in full swing at the town hall. Music, voices, and laughter drifted out into the moonlit night as Billy and his friends raced down the street.

When they finally stopped and looked back, they were relieved to find that the scary warlock was nowhere in sight. The only one behind them was Frankendude.

"Hey, Mr. Carroll," Billy called to him, "maybe you can help us find—"

But Frankendude didn't let him finish. "Give me staaaaaffffff!" he cried in a chilling voice.

Billy gulped. He'd just noticed Frankendude's glowing green eyes. He ducked as Frankendude grabbed for the staff. The monster tripped over the pumpkin on his foot and crashed into some Halloween decorations.

"Frankendude sure is taking his role seriously," Pete commented.

Sam nodded. "He's not normal, even for Mr. Carroll."

"Let's go to the party," Alice suggested. "Sheriff Dan is in there."

The group hurried into the town hall.

Frankendude clambered to his feet and lumbered after them.

Hoot was flying overhead. When Warwick caught up, the owl glided down.

"They went in there, Master," he said, nodding toward the town hall.

Warwick stared at the building. Strange lights and sounds were coming from inside.

"This must be that young warlock's lair," Warwick said. "It's swarming with those creatures."

Just then a group of kids came by. One of them, dressed in a devil costume, tugged on Warwick's robe.

"Trick or treat!" the boy said. "Hand over your loot."

"Aah!" Warwick cried in fear. "Back

away, demon! You'll not trick-or-treat me!"

He grabbed one of the creature's horns in self-defense. But both horns were attached to a headband, which came off in his hand. Warwick stared at it in confusion.

"You are no demon!" he exclaimed.

He reached over and grabbed the mask off another kid's face.

"And you're no goblin!" he added. "What is this trickery? They're just kids in disguise!"

"Halloween is not like it used to be," Hoot explained to the warlock. "It's all about candy and costumes."

"Costumes?!" Warwick cried. "So that boy warlock is just a boy? Why didn't

you tell me that, you birdbrain? Let's get him!" And with that, he headed straight into the town hall.

Moments after Warwick disappeared into the party, the Buddies arrived at the town hall. They hurried around the building until they found Deputy Sniffer standing guard.

"Deputy Sniffer, wake up!" Rosebud yelped. "We need your help!"

"What's the problem?" Sniffer asked with a yawn. "Did someone steal Budderball's candy bag?"

"No," Zelda said. "This is more serious than trick-or-treating."

B-Dawg nodded. "The Howlloween Hound has been released!"

Deputy Sniffer rolled his eyes. He assumed the puppies were playing a prank on him. Then Pip floated in front of him.

"Wow, great ghost costume!" Sniffer said, impressed.

"It's not a costume, Deputy Sniffer," Zelda said. "He's a ghost."

Deputy Sniffer raised his eyebrows. He clearly didn't believe Zelda. So, to prove it, Pip flew through the wall of the town hall and then came back.

Deputy Sniffer's ears stood on end. "Well, I'll be a doggone dog!" he exclaimed in surprise.

"I knew your great grand-pappy, Deputy Tracker," Pip told him. "He did his best to save us. Now, we could really use your help."

Just then, Sniffer looked up in alarm. "Would this Hound happen to be large and brown and racing toward us?" he asked.

The puppies turned around to look. The Hound was running right for them!

"Oh, no!" Zelda yelped. "He's found us!"

"What do we do?" B-Dawg cried.

"The long paw of the law will handle this intruder," Sniffer said. "You guys go."

The Buddies, Zelda, and Pip took off. Deputy Sniffer bravely faced down the Howlloween Hound.

"Stop, in the name of the law!" he ordered as the Hound reached him. "Those pups are under my protection."

But the Hound just laughed evilly.

Then he began to howl. A green glow poured out of his mouth. It surrounded Sniffer—and then turned him to stone!

At the party, Sheriff Dan was judging the costume contest.

When the kids arrived, Billy ran up to the sheriff. The boy still held the staff in his hand. "Sheriff Dan," he cried, "I've got to talk to you!"

"With you in a jiffy, Billy," Sheriff Dan said. "Got to announce our winner." He turned to the crowd. "And the first prize goes to . . . Frank Carroll for Frankendude!"

The audience cheered loudly. But Frankendude looked confused.

Then he spotted Billy standing in front of the stage. *Aha!* Now he remembered why he was here.

Frankendude lunged toward Billy, trying to grab the staff. But Mrs. Carroll stepped in front of him with a camera.

"Say cheese!" she said.

The flash of the camera momentarily blinded Frankendude's green eyes. He tripped over his pumpkin foot and fell off the stage, landing on Warwick.

"Get off me, you buffoon!" Warwick cried.

"Sheriff," Billy said through the commotion. "It's important!"

But Warwick had managed to pick himself up. "Give that staff to me, boy!" Warwick yelled. "It belongs to me—

Warwick, the greatest warlock of all time!" He grabbed the staff.

"Hey!" Billy yelled. "I have to return that to Sheriff Dan!"

"Now, what have you done with my book?" Warwick demanded, seizing Billy by the robe.

"Hey, now," Sheriff Dan said. "That isn't proper party etiquette, sir. I'll need you to put the boy down. No more of this monkey business."

Warwick smirked. "Monkey business, eh?" He pointed his staff at the sheriff. *"Transformus primatus!"*

The jewel on the staff glowed. Then a flash of light shot out, and Sheriff Dan was transformed into a monkey! He was even wearing a tiny police uniform.

"What in tarnation?" Sheriff Dan the monkey said. "You're under arrest for insulting an officer of the law! No one makes a monkey out of Sheriff Dan!"

The partygoers watched in awe. They clearly all thought this was an act. "Great trick!" exclaimed Billy's mom. "Just fabulous!"

Billy decided it was time to run. Warwick saw him, and with a quick spell, he burst out of the crowd by floating into the air on his staff. The partygoers cheered even louder at that.

"Thank you, thank you! It's great to be loved," Warwick said. Then he smiled an evil smile. "But better to be feared."

And with that, he took off after Billy.

Chapter Ten

Billy found his friends outside the town hall.

"Dude," Pete said. "Did you give Sheriff Dan the staff?"

"Sort of . . ." Billy replied.

Just then, Sheriff Dan the monkey raced out of the building. Bartleby stared at him.

"That monkey is dressed like Sheriff Dan," he commented.

"Run, kids!" the monkey cried. "He's coming!"

Warwick floated out, standing on his staff. "There you are!" he snarled, spotting Billy. "Now where's the book? Or do you all want to end up as monkeys, too?"

"Really, mister," Billy said, frightened. "We don't know where it is."

"Wrong answer, boy." Warwick pointed his staff. *"Transformus prim—"*

Before he could finish, a shovel conked him on the head. He tumbled to the ground, stunned.

The kids gasped when they saw who was holding the shovel. It was Mr. Johnson from the cemetery!

"Come with me," Mr. Johnson told them.

The kids weren't sure what to do. Mr. Johnson was pretty spooky. But Warwick was even spookier. And he was already getting up.

The gang ran after Mr. Johnson. He led them to a hearse parked nearby.

The kids all jumped in. Mr. Johnson got in the driver's seat and hit the gas.

A few minutes later, the hearse pulled up in front of a church.

"We'll be safe here. Evil like Warwick cannot enter the house of God.

"Quickly, everyone inside," Mr. Johnson directed. He spotted Warwick flying toward them on his staff. "It's our only chance."

"How come you have a key?" Alice asked.

"I'm the organist here every Sunday," Mr. Johnson said. "Don't worry, kids. We beat Warwick before. We can do it again."

Once everyone was in the church, Billy pulled out the photograph from the police files. "This is you, isn't it?" he asked. "You're the boy from the legend."

Mr. Johnson looked at the photo. "That sure was a long time ago. . . ."

Outside, Warwick landed and swiftly walked up to the church. "I need that book," he said to himself. He pointed his staff at the door. *"Openus sesamus!"*

The jewel glowed and fired a magical beam. But the beam hit the church door and bounced back at Warwick.

Mr. Johnson had been right, the church

really did protect against black magic.

Inside, Mr. Johnson pulled a package out of a hiding place in the church organ. He removed the dusty wrappings to reveal a spell book.

"For seventy-five years I've held on to this book, dreading a full moon on Halloween night," he told the kids.

"He will need to complete the spell tonight for the evil spirits of the netherworld to remain here."

"The nether what, now?" Billy asked, confused.

"It's another name for the place where ghosts live," Mr. Johnson told him. "Usually bad ones. Halloween is the one night these spirits can roam free in our world. Only the Howlloween Hound can call them out. Warwick will use the spirits to control the townsfolk of Fernfield."

The kids were scared. "He needs to complete the spell?" Alice asked.

"That's right," Mr. Johnson said. "Warwick must have his staff, the spell book, and one other thing."

"What is it?" Billy asked.

Mr. Johnson looked grim. "The souls of five puppies who share the same blood."

"Like brothers and sisters?" Alice asked.

She and her friends looked at one another. "The Buddies!" they all said.

At that moment, the Buddies, Pip, and Zelda were at the cemetery searching for Pip's earthly body.

"Could this night get any creepier?" Mudbud asked, glancing around the dark cemetery.

"Everyone look for Pip," Zelda instructed.

"There I am!" Pip cried, pointing his paw at a statue.

They all approached the stone puppy. Beside it was a metal sign.

"'Here stands Pip,'" Buddha read aloud. "'Most loyal friend of Joseph. The best pup a boy could ever have. One day, we'll be together again.'"

Rosebud glanced at Zelda. "What do we do now?"

Zelda looked uncertain. "I've never returned a spirit to a body, but I'll give it a whirl. All of you make a circle around

Pip's body. I'll need all your energies."

As the wind rustled the leaves on the trees, the Buddies gathered around. They didn't see the Howlloween Hound as he entered the cemetery and sniffed the air.

Hoot had been flying over the town, spying on everyone. He saw the Howlloween Hound sneaking up on the Buddies. So he flew back into town and told Warwick.

"Perfect!" Warwick was still peering in the church window. He had been listening to the kids' conversation. He hadn't known that both he *and* the Hound needed the Buddies. "I think those puppies are going to come in handy in more ways than one."

Chapter Eleven

The Buddies and Zelda gathered around the stone statue of Pip. Pip himself floated overhead.

"Help us, spirits," Zelda chanted. "Take this soul and place it back into the body the Hound once stole!"

She opened her eyes and looked up. Pip was glowing.

"It's working!" the ghost puppy said.

Zelda repeated the spell, faster this time. Then even faster.

As she did, Pip floated down toward his stone body. The Buddies watched in awe.

"It's really working!" Rosebud said.

Pip's spirit touched the statue, then sank into it. The stone softened and started to move.

"Whoa, guys," Pip said. "My legs . . ."

He shook his legs.

"My tail . . ."

He wagged his tail.

"I'm back!" he cried.

He spun in circles. He was so excited he couldn't stand still! Letting out a yip of joy, he dashed off into the graveyard.

A second later, the Hound came out from his hiding place. "This time there's nowhere to run, Buddies!" he snarled.

Pip raced back just in time to hear him. But the Hound didn't see him, so he hid behind a tree.

Zelda stepped forward, trying to block the Hound from getting to the Buddies. "No!" she said as fiercely as she could.

The Hound opened his mouth and howled. The Buddies watched in horror as Zelda turned to stone!

"We're doomed!" B-Dawg moaned.

The Hound took a deep breath, ready to howl again. But just then, Warwick and Hoot arrived.

"Not now, Hound. We need these puppies," Warwick told him. He trapped the Buddies with a freezing spell so they couldn't run away. Then he laughed wickedly. "Now all I need is the book."

And he had a plan to get it.

"These puppies belong to those pesky kids. They will try to rescue them. Hound, take the puppies to thc manor and wait for me." And with that, Warwick sped back to the church on his staff.

"You in there!" he called from outside the church. "I have something of yours." He waited a moment, and then the doors opened. Mr. Johnson and the kids peered out.

"If you want to see your puppies again, you'd better bring that book to my manor," Warwick told them. Then he flew off.

"Oh, no, they've got the Buddies!" Alice cried.

Billy turned to Mr. Johnson. "What should we do?"

"I can't let what happened to Pip happen to your pups," Mr. Johnson said. "We must save them and put an end to Warwick once and for all."

Pip had followed the Hound and the Buddies back to the manor. Now he sneaked in through the front door of the house.

Upstairs in the turret room, the Buddies were locked in a cage. The Hound was guarding them while Hoot looked on.

"Soon I will swallow all of your souls,"

the Hound told the Buddies, licking his lips. "I can't wait."

Budderball looked nervous. "Is it just me, or does this guy talk about eating more than I do?"

Just then, Warwick swooped in through the window. "Master, where have you been?" Hoot asked anxiously.

"I told those wretched children to bring me the spell book," Warwick replied.

"What if they don't?" Hoot asked.

"Quiet, you moronic birdbrain!" Warwick yelled. "They'll want to save their darling puppies, won't they?"

Pip made his way upstairs and peeked in through the doorway.

"Psst . . . Buddies!" he whispered.

"Pip!" Rosebud shot a nervous look at Warwick, but the warlock wasn't looking at them.

"We need a distraction to get you out of here," Pip whispered. "I'll be right back!"

He backed away from the door, trying to figure out how to distract Warwick. Just then a pair of rats raced by, followed by a black cat. *Aha!* That gave Pip an idea. He took off after them.

The rats ducked into a hole in the wall. The cat crouched outside, waiting to pounce.

Pip peered into the hole. "I need your help," he told the rats. He believed they were humans who had been turned into rodents by Warwick. And he was right. The rats were Rodney and Skip!

"What's in it for us?" Rodney the rat replied.

"First of all, I won't let that cat eat you as a Halloween treat," Pip said.

"Eat *him*!" Skip the rat said quickly. "He's plumper."

"You are such a rat!" Rodney told him.

"More importantly," Pip said, "if we don't break the warlock's spell tonight, you'll be rats forever."

Rodney and Skip didn't like the sound of that. Being rats wasn't much fun.

"Okay," Rodney said. "We'll help."

"Wise decision," Pip said.

He convinced the cat to leave the rats alone. Then he led Rodney and Skip to the turret. They scurried in, staying close to the walls.

Warwick didn't see the rats coming. He was staring intently out the window. Mr. Johnson's hearse had just pulled up outside.

"Perfect," Warwick told the Hound. "Soon I'll have my spell book, and then you can devour those delicious puppy souls."

Suddenly he felt something crawling up the inside of his pant leg. He let out a yelp.

"What is it?" the Hound asked, startled.

"Something is biting me!" Warwick cried. "Hound, Hoot, do something!"

He danced around the room shaking and wiggling, trying to get the rats off him.

"That dawg has some serious moves,"

B-Dawg commented. He could definitely appreciate dance skills.

Finally Warwick shook the rats out of his robes.

"Change us back!" Skip demanded.

"I'm going to get you filthy vermin!" Warwick cried as the rats scurried away. "No one bites me! Hound, catch them and they're yours to eat. I'll go get that book from those stupid kids."

"Our kids are here?" Rosebud perked up her ears. "Oh, no!"

"Hoot, guard the puppies," Warwick ordered. "Fail me, and I'll make you into a feather duster."

"Yes, Master," Hoot said as Warwick and the Hound rushed out of the room.

Chapter Twelve

Pip waited until the coast was clear and then sneaked over to the Buddies.

He tried to unlock the cage, but Hoot spotted him.

"*Hoo! Hoo!* Stop!" he hooted. "What do you think you're doing?"

"Saving my friends," Pip said.

Hoot shook his head. "I can't let them escape."

"Hoot, why are you so loyal to Warwick?" Rosebud asked.

"Seriously, dude," Mudbud said. "It's totally obvious he plans to get rid of you."

"Master sometimes gets angry," Hoot said. "But he would never get rid of me. He needs me!"

"He's got that Howlloween Hound to do his dirty work now," B-Dawg told the owl. "He calls you names like 'moronic birdbrain.'"

Hoot nodded. "That does sound like something he'd say."

"I know that you never meant to hurt me, Hoot," Pip said. "I'm Pip, the ghost dog. Haven't the last seventy years without evil been a lot nicer than your time under Warwick's wing?"

Hoot looked thoughtful. "It *was*

kind of nice not having to look over my shoulder all the time," he said. "Even though that's quite easy for me."

To demonstrate, he turned his head all the way around. Warwick and the Hound were still nowhere in sight. So Hoot hopped down and used one of his claws to pick the lock on the cage.

Pip smiled. "You won't regret it, Hoot. I promise."

Rodney and Skip raced through the manor with the Hound on their tails. They made it to their hiding hole just in time.

The Hound skidded to a stop. "I've had enough of chasing you measly morsels anyway," he growled. He was ready for the puppies.

The Hound headed back to the turret room. When he walked in, he saw that the Buddies were out of their cage.

"How did you get out?" he demanded.

"Hound! Over here!" Pip called. "It's me—Pip. You stole my sister's and all my brothers' souls, and you only needed mine. The spell was broken before you got my soul."

"I remember you," the Hound said.

"Then take me and let the Buddies go," Pip said bravely. "Take me, and you'll have five souls of the same blood."

The Buddies watched in horror as the Hound nodded. "You make a sound proposal," he told Pip. "I agree."

He opened his mouth and howled.

"No, dude!" Mudbud cried. "Don't!"

"Good-bye, Buddies," Pip said.

A second later, he was stone again.

"The final soul is mine!" the Hound growled in delight. He stepped over to the mirror. "Open the portal! Release the evil spirits!"

He howled at the mirror. The dark glass glowed. Strange, ghostly spirits started to fly out of it. They headed straight for the town to put curses on all the townspeople.

The Hound watched for a moment, then turned to the Buddies. "Now," he said, "to take five more puppy souls."

"You promised to let them go!" Hoot reminded him.

"I lied," the Hound said.

Hoot couldn't believe it. And he

couldn't let this happen! He flew at the Hound to stop him. The Hound howled, and Hoot turned to stone and fell to the floor with a thud.

But he'd distracted the Hound just long enough for the Buddies to run out of the room.

The Buddies raced down the stairs, heading for the front door. Suddenly Warwick stepped into view!

Mudbud looked back. The Hound was at the top of the stairs behind them.

"Dudes, we're trapped!" he cried.

But Rosebud didn't panic. "This way," she said, leading them through a door off the stair landing.

"Hound!" Warwick yelled. "Get those puppies, now!"

The Buddies found themselves in a parlor with dusty furniture and a fireplace. There were no other doors.

"Great, dawg," B-Dawg said. "A dead end!"

The Hound bounded into the room. "I have you now!" he growled.

Suddenly, the rats Rodney and Skip appeared by the fireplace. "This way, puppies!" Rodney called.

The Buddies hurried over. The rats pushed a button, and the fireplace spun around, taking the Buddies with it!

Chapter Thirteen

Mr. Johnson and the kids walked toward the manor's front door. Mr. Johnson was holding a large book.

As they looked up, they saw strange lights flashing in the turret. Ghostly shapes flew out of the windows in every direction.

"Oh, no!" Mr. Johnson said. "They've opened the portal. Now all Warwick needs to do is complete the spell and it will remain open forever. All good will be overcome by evil. But we can still stop it." He took a large cross out of his coat. "Stay close to me, kids."

They had to find the Buddies before it was too late!

When they entered the manor, Warwick was waiting for them.

"We have your book," Mr. Johnson told him.

Warwick didn't want to waste any more time. The moon would be setting soon. "Hand it over," he ordered.

"Where are our Buddies?" Billy asked.

"Oh, they're around here some-where," Warwick said.

He reached for the book. But Mr.

Johnson held up the cross to stop him.

Warwick sighed. Why did nonevil people have to be so stubborn?

"As you wish," he said. "Follow me."

He flew up the stairs. Mr. Johnson and the kids followed Warwick into the turret room. "Where are the Buddies?" Billy asked.

"They were right here," Warwick said. "But you're too late."

He pointed his staff at Mr. Johnson and shot a beam of magical energy at him. The magic knocked Mr. Johnson off his feet. Warwick grabbed the book from him.

"Now I will finish the spell, and the creatures of the netherworld will be here forever! I will rule the land once and for all!" He cackled with glee and opened the book. "Wait a minute," he said, a confused look on his face. "This isn't my spell book!"

Taking advantage of the warlock's surprise, Mr. Johnson grabbed Warwick's staff and tossed it to Billy. "Billy—the spell!"

"My staff!" Warwick howled, struggling to get past Mr. Johnson.

Billy pulled the real spell book out of his backpack and opened it. *"Protectus!"* he chanted.

The staff fired a magical beam at Warwick, knocking him back.

Meanwhile, the Buddies were trying to sneak out of the manor. But the Hound caught up to them in the kitchen.

"That's it, you miserable pups," he growled. "Nowhere left to run! I'll have all your souls now."

Luckily, B-Dawg had an idea. "All right, dawg. You win," he said. "But take Budderball first. He's the plumpest."

The rest of the Buddies gasped.

"Silence!" the Hound ordered. "I don't care who's first."

"Trust me," B-Dawg whispered to the others. "I've got a plan."

"B-Dawg has a plan?" Rosebud whispered, surprised.

"I can have a plan!" B-Dawg said defensively.

The Hound began to howl. Magical green energy came out of his mouth and drifted toward Budderball.

But at that moment, B-Dawg started dancing. He spun and jumped and danced so furiously that all the dust that had built up in the house over the years came swirling into the air. The Hound started coughing.

"Ugh!" the Hound cried, trying to suck in some fresh air. But as he breathed in, the green magical energy got sucked back around him!

"No!" the Hound cried. "This can't be happening!"

But it was. The magic surrounded him—and before the puppies' eyes, the Hound turned to stone! The Buddies couldn't believe it!

"That was totally wicked!" Mudbud exclaimed.

B-Dawg smiled. He knew he had it in him.

In the turret room, Billy's spell was keeping Warwick away from him and his friends. But for how long?

"Hand me the staff, boy!" Warwick ordered.

"No!" Billy closed his eyes. He was scared out of his wits. Could he do what he needed to do next?

Mr. Johnson looked out the window. The sun was breaking over the horizon.

"Quick, Billy!" he urged. "The sun is rising. Say the spell!"

Billy held up the staff. Sunlight bounced off it and hit the mirror nearby.

Just then the Buddies rushed in. But

Billy hardly saw them. He was focused on the spell book.

He read one of the spells out loud.

"To annul the spell and still the beast
And all that has been wrought release,
Turn about, and say it thrice:
All's as was in a trice."

"No!" Warwick yelled as Billy recited the last line of the spell.

The mirror lit up, and spirits came flying toward it from every direction. The mirror was sucking them in as if it were a magical vacuum!

Warwick fought the pull of the mirror. But it was too strong.

"Drat!" he cried. "Not again!"

He tried to grab Mr. Johnson. But the man stomped on the warlock's foot.

Warwick yelped in pain. All of a sudden he noticed that Mr. Johnson looked familiar. And that foot-stomping definitely *felt* familiar.

"It's you!" he exclaimed, realizing that Mr. Johnson was Joseph. "I'll take you with me this time!" He grabbed Mr. Johnson, dragging him toward the mirror.

"Mr. Johnson!" Billy yelled.

Just then, the stone statue of Pip came back to life, thanks to the power of Billy's spell. Pip saw what was happening and leaped forward, knocking Warwick and Mr. Johnson apart.

"Nooooo!" Warwick wailed.

The mirror grabbed the warlock and pulled him in. He clutched the edge, trying to stay free. But the magic was too strong. Warwick lost his grip and tumbled into the mirror, disappearing just as the magical light faded away.

A second later the room was normal again. Mr. Johnson looked down at Pip.

"You saved my life," he said.

Pip barked and jumped up joyfully.

Then there were several other barks. It was Pip's brothers and sister! Their stone forms had been sitting in the turret room all along. They'd come back to life, too!

Hoot also returned to normal. He hooted happily.

"Thank you, Hoot," Pip said. He

knew they couldn't have beaten Warwick without the owl's help. "Now my brothers and sis can be reunited with their kids, too."

All around town, the evil magic was reversed. Zelda and Deputy Sniffer returned to life. Sheriff Dan changed from a monkey back into a man. Rodney and Skip turned back into boys. All the townsfolk woke from their spells.

In the turret room, Mr. Johnson lifted the staff. He smashed it down on a table. The gem shattered. A moment later, a crack formed in the turret's mirror, then another. Finally the whole thing fell to pieces! Warwick would never be able to return.

Then Mr. Johnson picked up his

puppy, Pip. Pip licked his face happily, and Mr. Johnson smiled.

"Come on, everyone," he said. "Let's get out of this evil place."

Chapter Fourteen

Billy stood at the front of the classroom. Mr. Johnson, Pip, and the Buddies were at his side as he finished his history presentation.

"And so the evil warlock was sucked into the mirror, never to be seen again," he said. "And Joseph Johnson was finally reunited with his long-lost puppy, Pip. The curse of the Howlloween Hound has been lifted, and Fernfield is now safe forever."

The class applauded. Mrs. Carroll smiled.

"That was quite the story, Billy," she said.

"It's more than just a story, Mrs. C," Billy said. "It really happened. Just ask Rodney and Skip. They were total heroes. Right, guys?"

Rodney and Skip looked sheepish. "Every word of it," Skip said sarcastically. "Especially the part where we *didn't* get turned into rats."

"Well, that was a very thorough presentation, Billy," Mrs. Carroll said. "You get an A-plus for your efforts. Congratulations."

Later, the kids and the Buddies stood

beside an old van with Mr. Johnson and Pip. Mr. Johnson had packed up the car with his belongings.

"What are you going to do now?" Alice asked Mr. Johnson.

Mr. Johnson smiled. He looked much happier now.

"I tracked down the owners of Pip's brothers and sister," he said. "They live all over the country now, so we're going to visit them."

"It's great to have a new *leash* on life," Pip added jokingly. "But I'll miss you, Buddies."

"Yo, we'll catch you on the flip side, dawg," B-Dawg said.

"I think what my brother means," Buddha added, "is we'll never forget you."

Pip smiled. He would never forget the Buddies, either. With that, Mr. Johnson and Pip climbed into their van. As they drove off, the Buddies and kids waved good-bye. And above them all flew Hoot, very happy to be free—and especially happy that the Buddies had rid Fernfield of the curse of the Howlloween Hound once and for all.